The Adventures of Milo Chow:
Being Good Isn't Easy!

Written by Caroline E Rayfield

Illustrated by Jamie Jamandre

The Adventures of Milo Chow
Copyright © 2022 by Caroline E Rayfield

tellwell

Tellwell Talent
www.tellwell.ca

ISBN
978-0-2288-7768-4 (Hardcover)
978-0-2288-7767-7 (Paperback)

Dedication

This book is dedicated to Milo, our Chow, who lives on through these stories. And to my family for supporting my decision to bring him home.

Table of Contents

The Adventures of Milo Chow...

Milo Chow Finds His Forever Home

Milo was a handsome four month-old Chow Chow puppy. His black hair was as soft as cotton. He had big brown eyes that were the colour of milk chocolate and a long purple tongue that hung proudly from his mouth. This Chow was as cute as could be. All he needed was a home to call his own.

Milo Chow had once been part of a family, but when they discovered that he had special needs, his family decided it was time to give Milo up. No one had been able to figure out what was wrong with this little boy. He walked in circles and ran sideways. He couldn't walk up the stairs and needed help getting down. Lots of people wanted to help Milo find a new home where he could spend his days being spoiled by a loving new family. His life had just started. The pup's next stop would be in Toronto. And here is where this story begins . . .

* * * * *

Milo was gently placed in a crate containing his favourite blanket and stuffed toy. The crate was like a little Milo-sized house, where he would stay safe while on the plane travelling from Winnipeg, Manitoba, to Toronto, Ontario. Milo was too young to completely understand what was happening. All he knew was that he would be joining a rescue in Toronto. This rescue would help him to find a new home and get the care he needed. He wondered what his new life would be like. Milo curled up in a ball and drifted off to sleep. The young pup slept deeply during the flight, comforted by the gentle swaying of the plane in the air.

It was still early in the morning when the plane landed at the Pearson International Airport in Toronto. The airport was very quiet. Milo was allowed out of his crate to stretch his legs and have a look around. He looked over and saw a lady approaching him. The woman greeted the Chow's travel escort first, and then greeted the puppy. She was the owner of the rescue that Milo would be joining. She was very gentle with him and he trusted her immediately. It wouldn't be long before he would be in his new home. Milo loved and missed his family but was curious about his new people.

Milo was placed back in his crate, which was then put into the car. A thin blanket of snow covered the ground. The air was crisp. Milo was happy that he had a thick coat to keep him warm. He curled up inside his crate and dozed off to sleep. The motion of the car was comforting and he dreamt of life with a new family.

After thirty minutes, the car stopped. Milo's door opened and a hand reached in to bring him out. He was sleepy from his nap but the cold air quickly woke him up. He was led into a tall building, which was where the owner of the rescue lived. They stepped into the elevator and it took them to her floor. When the door opened, out they stepped. In front of them was a narrow hallway leading to her home. She swung the door open and a black-and-tan dog with pointy ears appeared before them. Her name was Destiny. She would be his first real friend. Destiny was a little bossy but he didn't mind. A few minutes after arriving, a bowl of food was put down in front of the pup and he began to eat. The food was delicious. He watched as his friend came closer and closer until there was a loud whistle. The older dog halted instantly and retreated back to her bed.

Milo finished his meal and began to wander from room to room. He knew that it wouldn't be too long before he got to meet his new foster family and he couldn't wait! After they were rested from their early morning start, they got back into the elevator and made their way down to the main floor. It was time to meet his foster mum. He was placed back into the crate and off they went. Fortunately, the rescue was only a few minutes away and Milo was able to stretch his legs again. He looked through the window and couldn't believe his eyes. They had arrived at a store, and a toy store no less! The door was pushed open and Milo stepped in. He looked around. It wasn't a toy store after all—it was a pet store. A woman immediately walked up to him. Before he knew it, he was scooped up into her arms. He liked her. Milo learned that her name was Caroline. He hoped that she would be his new mum. He loved how she stroked his back and patted his head. His eyes closed and he drifted off to sleep. He was only a baby Chow; no one would blame him for needing his sleep. Milo could hear the muffled sounds of a conversation happening behind him. He could hear that something bad had happened and he was right. It was bad news. His foster had backed out . . . he had no place to go.

Still in Caroline's arms, Milo heard the words, "I will take him. Milo will come home with me." The Chow wasn't sure what was happening. He was put back into the carrier and placed into a different car. He heard the sound of items being sorted in the car next to him. This was all very curious. Where was he going?

After a twenty-minute drive, the car stopped and the door opened. A whoosh of cold air blew straight through him. This was a new place. Milo was nervous but he felt safe in Caroline's arms. They stepped through the front door. He knew where he was. He was home.

The Adventures of Milo Chow...

Milo Chow Gets a New Family

13

Milo was carried up the three stairs that led into his new home. From the outside, the house looked small. He was curious about what lay behind the doors. Caroline held on to the Chow tightly so that he wouldn't fall. They entered the enclosed porch, where his leash was taken off and hung up on one of the four hooks that were attached to the wall. He noticed that there were three other leashes hanging next to his. One was pink; the other two were blue and green. Did he really need four leashes? This day was getting better and better. He would be the coolest Chow the world had ever seen. There were big things in store for Milo. He just knew it.

The front door opened. A young girl appeared and then another. A dog raced by them, and then a second and a third. He soon realised that the extra leashes were not for him but for the other three dogs. Milo always wanted a big family and he finally had one! The girl dog hopped around him, looking at Milo from all sides. She introduced herself as Dominica. Dominica was beautiful with large blue eyes and pointy ears. He noticed that something was wrong with her back legs but decided not to ask about them. Dominica's brother, Sully, raced up to him. He was fast and had a loud bark. It frightened the little Chow. Milo looked behind them to see a little tan-and-grey dog. He introduced himself as Oliver. Just like Destiny, Oliver was bossy. Very bossy.

Milo wondered about his new brothers and sisters. He was so lucky to have dog siblings and human siblings. He was certain there must be hundreds of them, but he hadn't learned to count so he couldn't be sure. There were decorations everywhere. Balloons covered the ceiling and music played in the background. Milo was thrilled. He never expected his new family to throw a party for him. How did they even know that he was coming? Suddenly, there was a knock at the front door followed by a series of loud barks. One of the children opened the door. There were more girls standing there with presents in their hands. Caroline took Milo aside. *Were they his sisters too?* he wondered. She explained to the pup that she was throwing a birthday party for one of her daughters. Milo was quickly surrounded by the girls who held him and patted him. The Chow Chow felt very happy and very lucky.

As the days passed, Milo began to feel more settled. The fear of returning to his old life slowly faded and he felt at home. He stopped thinking of Caroline as his foster mum and started to believe that she was his real mum. Milo loved her and he knew that she loved him. He loved the games they played together and was always very happy when she came home from her volunteer work at the rescue. Caroline often returned with a treat for her other dogs. Milo always got a new toy. He wasn't ready for treats yet. The puppy couldn't wait to become a big boy like his brothers.

Milo loved mealtimes. He would wait patiently alongside Oliver, Sully and Dominica. Caroline would carefully place their bowls on the counter and, one by one, fill each with yummy food. Dominica and Sully had food for medium-sized dogs, Oliver got food for small dogs and Milo got puppy food. One day he hoped that they could all eat the same food. He didn't want to get in trouble for sneaking a mouthful of anyone else's food. Milo was very proud of the fact that he had never been told off by his mum.

The day finally arrived when Milo was able to eat the same food as his siblings. It was a very exciting day! Although Milo was still a pup, his mum had found a new food for all four dogs. It looked like hamburger. Milo tried a tiny bite. It was very delicious. The Chow's whole head was in his bowl, and with every bite his head flew back in delight. The young pup looked just like Cookie Monster with food flying in all directions. Milo licked his face and then the floor to ensure that every last piece was eaten.

Milo learned new things with each passing day. For example, he learned that it was better to pee outside and not on the living room floor. He learned that his sister Dominica was not okay with him standing right next to her while she ate. He also learned to wrestle with his big brother Sully. Sometimes he enjoyed standing in the middle while Sully and Dominica wrestled. Little by little, Milo was growing up.

It wasn't long before Milo became the centre of their family. Oliver, Dominica and Sully doted on him. As a family they celebrated every new month with Milo. It was a cause for celebration. Every day was cherished. This young boy was very happy with his new life. He couldn't wait to see what tomorrow would bring!

Milo was happy. Life was good for this Chow.

The Adventures of Milo Chow...

Milo Chow Gets His Wish

It was late afternoon when Caroline returned home from her work at the rescue. Milo noticed that his mum was holding a brown paper bag. He sniffed the bag for a clue. The more he sniffed, the more excited he got. He had hoped every day for one thing . . . a brand-new ball that was just his. Milo would not be sharing his ball. Everyone knew that the baby of the family didn't have to share.

The bag was placed gently on the ground and Milo peered inside. He could hardly believe his eyes. His wish had come true! Inside the bag was the most perfect ball that Milo had ever seen. He always loved when a ball was thrown for him to chase. The pup tried to bring it straight back to her but sometimes chewing it was far more fun. Milo knew that he was very fast chasing his ball, but he never trusted that Sully wouldn't jump out and grab it.

One Saturday morning, Caroline threw the ball. Milo looked and looked but couldn't find it. At first he thought this might be part of the game. He soon realised that the most awful thing that could ever happen to a little Chow had happened— his ball had disappeared! He tried not to cry but he couldn't help it. Milo looked up at his mum and cried. He wanted his ball back. Milo was scooped up into her arms and quickly brought into the house. Within minutes, she had locked the back door and was in the car, heading straight for the pet store. There would be no unhappy Chows in her house today.

Caroline parked the car and raced into the store. She picked up three balls that were identical to his missing ball. Milo's mum would take no chance ever again that he would have to go without his favourite ball. Listening to her puppy cry was unbearable for her! Caroline drove home with the three new balls. She unlocked the back door and called for Milo. He had been waiting for her. Milo had figured out that by crying he could get anything he wanted. He was a very smart Chow Chow. He was lifted into her arms and carried into the garden. Milo was a happy boy again.

The pup spent most of his days chasing the ball. His mum would take lots of videos of him running to show the other rescue mums and dads. The Chow knew how proud she was of his progress. Milo liked to show off by running as fast as he could and chomping down on his ball.

Milo also enjoyed waking up very early in the morning to have his mum throw his toy. He would let out a whimper and Caroline would get up and carry him outside to play with the ball. Milo loved this game. Playing in the dark was lots of fun, even if his mum was grumpy from having been woken up.

For her birthday, Caroline bought a beautiful garden bench that she would sit on while Milo played with his ball. She named the bench, "Milo's Bench." He loved that a whole bench was named after him. Mum was right. He must be very special. Milo was happy. He loved his ball as much as he loved his family. Well, almost as much.

Life was good for this Chow.

The Adventures of Milo Chow...

Milo Meets His Shadow

Milo Chow had been with his family for several months. He was growing from a tiny black ball of fluff into a very handsome young boy. His hair was growing and he was gaining weight. He was thriving in his new home. Milo was a very happy Chow. Long gone were the memories of his life in Manitoba. He was a city boy and he had the world in his paws.

Milo really loved going on walks. He loved breathing in the fresh air and looking at all of the sights around him. The only problem was that Milo was not one for taking long walks. He would look up at his mum and cry. This was the sign that Milo was ready to be carried. He could then lie back in her arms with his legs fully outstretched and look at everything around him. Milo was turning into quite a heavy boy, so after a while his mum would have to place him back on the ground. This would repeat a number of times during their walks, with Milo walking for a few minutes then looking up at her, letting out a small cry, and being scooped up into her arms.

The day arrived that Milo had grown too big to be carried anymore. It was a very sad day for both of them. Milo loved being in his mummy's arms and Caroline loved carrying her little pup like a baby.

One morning when the sun was shining, Milo looked down at the ground. He noticed a figure that seemed to move in front of him. He was very curious. The shape looked just like him and even walked at the same speed. When Milo stopped, the figure also stopped. Caroline could see that Milo had discovered his shadow. The Chow was confused by the shape walking with him. He walked faster to investigate. The young pup barked at the shadow in an attempt to get it to stop moving. The puppy was growing frustrated. He stopped walking so he could think for a minute. The shadow also stopped. It was teasing the young Chow Chow. Milo decided that he would try to catch this shadow. He ran as fast as he could in an attempt to pounce on it. The shadow seemed to know what Milo was thinking and quickly moved. Milo sighed and continued to walk with Caroline holding his leash. He would have to figure out a plan for this shadow.

The following day, Milo stood at the doorway that led from the porch. It was another sunny day and he was excited to go on his walk. By this time he had forgotten all about the events of the previous day. Caroline carried her six-month-old pup down the steps and gently placed him on the ground. They set off through the front gate. As soon as they reached the front path, Milo looked down and saw the pesky shadow. Today would be the day that he caught this little pest. Milo chased and chased his shadow but never caught it. After a short time had passed, he realised that he had started to enjoy this game. Walk after walk, Milo would look for his little friend, the shadow, and their game would begin.

The day came when there was no sun shining down on them. Dark clouds filled the sky. There would be no game today. The shadow was nowhere to be seen. Milo refused to walk. It was a sad day. A very sad day. Caroline lifted the Chow down the steps and again placed him on the ground. Milo did not move. He looked up at her and then back at the house. He wanted to go home. He was not a happy Chow. Caroline lifted Milo back into her arms and began their walk. Milo stretched out his little legs and lay back. He looked at the overcast sky and thought of his shadow. Milo would see his friend again when the sunshine returned.

   This Chow was happy to have found his shadow. Life was good.

The Adventures of Milo Chow...

Milo Chow and the Great Chase

Milo Chow was always searching for a new game to play while he was on his walk. Being a young pup, he tended to get bored easily. A new game was always needed to keep him walking. Once the Chow Chow was bored he would refuse to walk. Milo was a big boy and the thought of carrying him gave his mum a backache.

It was a cool morning in late April when Milo and Caroline decided to go for a short walk. The front door opened slightly and it was clear that Milo would need to wear his favourite red coat. He loved this coat. It was the second one that Milo had been given since arriving in Toronto. The first had been a blue fleece coat that the rescue had given to him when he first arrived. The pup knew that he looked very cute in his jacket, often being told so by people walking by. There were frequently people who had treats in their pockets and Milo knew that looking cute was the best way to get one of those treats.

The Chow Chow stepped into his coat and he was zipped up. The leash was attached to his collar and they were ready to go. The door was pushed open and Caroline carried her boy down the steps and onto the ground. Despite the wind blowing, Milo stayed warm. He did not love how the wind blew his hair forward making it look like he was wearing earmuffs.

As they crossed the road, the Chow noticed that the breeze was causing leaves to scatter. One leaf actually blew into his face! He quickly chomped down on the leaf, mashing it with his teeth. His head bobbed back and forth as he devoured it, the Chow Chow looked just like a giant bobblehead. Milo felt very proud of himself.

A second leaf flew in front of him. The pup ran quickly to try and catch it. The leaf was too fast for young Milo and it blew straight into the road. The Chow darted after it. Caroline was not happy that Milo had run into the road. Even on a leash, Milo could have been hurt if a car or bike had been passing by. Caroline warned him in a stern voice that they would go home if he tried to go into the road after a leaf again. The pup looked up at his mum with his beautiful brown eyes. It was difficult to stay upset with such a sweet little face.

Milo learned to catch leaves without going into the road. He would run as quickly as he could, pouncing like a cat until he had caught his prey. The Chow would look at his mum with the stem of the leaf sticking out from his mouth. Sometimes he would walk for a while with one leaf stuffed into his mouth. He savoured that one leaf until it was time for a big chomp, and the leaf would fall from his mouth in tiny little pieces.

Caroline waited until Milo was ready to go home, and they slowly strolled in the direction of their home. It had been a successful day. Milo had a new game that he loved.

Milo was a happy Chow. Life was good.

The Adventures of Milo Chow...

Milo Chow and Dominica Rule the World

When Milo had grown old enough to walk well on his leash, Caroline decided that it was time for him to have a walking partner. She had the perfect dog for the job: Milo's big sister, Dominica. Dominica enjoyed slow walks. She liked to look at all of the sights and smell everything. Milo was a happy-go-lucky little boy. He would happily follow his sister. Caroline was counting on this.

The sky was overcast on the first morning that Dominica and Milo would walk together. Dominica hesitated before stepping down onto the first step. She did not like the rain and an overcast sky meant that rain was on its way. Milo was carried down the three front steps and lowered to the ground. They waited for Dominica to decide whether she would be joining them. Dominica was as stubborn as they came. If she wasn't happy, no one was happy. Upon seeing her little brother waiting, Dominica made her way down onto the next step. This was progress. Caroline held her breath that Dominica would continue down the steps. Thankfully she did. They would be able to have their walk.

As the three stood at the edge of the sidewalk, Dominica looked up the street. She was planning their route. This was her job on every walk. She took a minute and then led Milo and Caroline across the street. Dominica was in no mood to walk up the hill today. If it started to rain, she would need to be able to run home. Quickly.

They had only been outside for a minute when the first drop of rain fell. Caroline encouraged Milo and Dominica to keep walking. Dominica was ready to turn back. Milo didn't mind getting wet, even though his hair got very poofy once it dried. Milo nudged Dominica forward. She was not amused. She let out a small growl to show her displeasure. Milo took a step back. He would let her lead the way. Dominica moved forward. She knew that the faster they moved, the faster she would be able to climb back into her bed with a treat. Dominica started to walk much faster, too fast for the little Chow. He stopped immediately. This was not okay with him. Milo wanted to be carried. The rain was now falling quite heavily. They were getting soaked. Caroline knew that in a minute she would have two dogs who refused to walk – that would be a huge problem. Dominica and Milo really enjoyed their food and they were both quite heavy. Caroline scooped up the Chow and walked his sister as fast as she could. Dominica stopped and looked back at her house. This was enough for one day. She changed directions and headed back home. Milo, who had scored a ride in his mum's arms, relaxed. He was perfectly content.

Once the three got back to the house, Dominica shook all of the rain out of her hair. Milo was dried with a towel and now looked twice his normal size due to his poofy hair. They enjoyed a snack and settled in for a long nap. It had been a very eventful first walk together. Milo was looking forward to their next one.

Milo and Dominica were happy. Life was good.

The Adventures of Milo Chow...

Milo Chow Meets a Giant

Milo loved lying in the covered porch with the front door wide open. He would rest on the small mat that his family used to wipe their feet. The porch was the window to the world for the young pup. Sometimes his sister and brothers would join him. They loved to sit quietly, waiting for people and their dogs to pass. As soon as they were close enough, the dogs would all bark as loudly as they could. Milo loved watching this. The passersby would jump into the air. Oliver, Sully and Dominica would then head back into the house, leaving Milo Chow to continue daydreaming.

The little Chow Chow loved watching dogs walk by his home. He often wished that he could run out and say hello. There were so many dogs that he had yet to meet. Having two brothers and a sister was wonderful, but Milo longed to have another friend that was just his.

Milo woke up earlier than usual one late spring morning. He wanted to have some time with his mum before the others got up. Milo ate his breakfast, licked up all the crumbs from the floor, and then headed to the front door. Caroline connected the leash to his collar and unlocked the glass door. The air was warm and there was a gentle breeze. Milo was carried down the three front steps and lowered to the ground. They made their way through the front gate and across the street. There were people with their dogs walking through the neighbourhood. Milo loved these early morning walks. He didn't have to compete for his mother's attention. Being a happy Chow was very, very important to Milo. In fact, it was his number one priority.

At the end of their street, they turned right and slowly proceeded to walk up a gradual hill. Just as Milo and Caroline turned the corner, they bumped into the biggest, hairiest giant that Milo had ever seen. He immediately darted behind his mother's legs. If anyone was going to be eaten by this huge creature, it wouldn't be him. Milo was only a baby Chow with plenty of years ahead of him!

Caroline stopped walking, Milo stayed safely behind her. The dog and his person were strangers to him and the pup was feeling very uncertain. The Chow's mum started to talk. She had clearly met them before. Maybe with Dominica. Milo was curious. Perhaps this giant wasn't as scary as he had originally thought. Milo crept out from behind Caroline's legs to get a better look. Little by little, the puppy inched closer to the giant ball of fur that stood in front of him. Caroline bent down so that she was closer to the Chow. She told Milo not to be frightened, Gus was a gentle giant. Milo sniffed him and could tell that he had just been bathed. The little Chow Chow really liked that smell.

Shortly afterwards, Milo felt the familiar tug on his leash. It was time to continue their walk. This time, Gus and his dad joined them. Milo worked hard to keep up with his new friend. He noticed that Gus had a slight limp. The Chow knew that it wasn't polite to stare so he would glance over from time to time to get a better look. Gus must be special like Milo and Dominica. He loved being special and loved that his new friend was just like him.

As was often the case with a long walk, Milo grew very sleepy. He wanted his mum to carry him home. The Chow let out a cry. Everyone looked at him. His mum would have to pick him up now. Once in her arms, Milo was able to peer over at Gus. They continued for a few minutes more before arriving back home. Gus walked a few houses down and up his own front steps.

Milo was happy that he not only had a new friend, but a new neighbour also. Life was good.

The Adventures
of Milo Chow...

Milo Chow Gets a Job

Milo's mum volunteered every Saturday at the rescue that had saved his life. Caroline loved her work there but found it very difficult spending four hours once a week away from her pup. Milo really missed her when she was away and her children complained that he spent the entire time crying for her. How could she leave him knowing how sad it made him? She decided that Milo would have a job at the rescue.

It was early on a Saturday morning that Caroline took Milo for his walk. It would be Milo's first time back at the rescue in a few months. He was excited to work with his mum. Today he had a very important job to do. He would be the store mascot. Milo knew that his job made him special. He was getting more special with each passing minute.

Travelling with the pup required some planning. Milo needed his food and water dishes, his favourite orange-and-blue ball, and lots of snacks. It was always important to make sure Milo was well fed. A full Milo was a happy Milo. Caroline put on his leash and collar and walked to the back door. Sully, Dominica and Oliver all stood watching as their mum and baby brother left.

Milo was quite comfortable sitting in the car. He liked sitting in the back seat looking out of his window. The window was rolled down just enough to let him feel a breeze but not too much that his hair got messed up. The Chow was so excited. He couldn't wait to get there. He knew that before they went into the rescue, they would first stop at the park across the street. They arrived a few minutes later and Caroline lowered Milo to the ground. This was going to be the best day ever!

After a quick stop at the park, Milo and his mum unlocked the glass door that led into the rescue and walked in. Milo's leash was removed and he immediately went into the other room. The rescue had a store that was attached to it. They sold pet supplies which Milo enjoyed looking at. The store was due to open in a few minutes. The puppy was bursting with excitement. He loved meeting the customers.

Milo picked up his ball. He wanted to be ready for the first customer. He would let them roll the ball for him to chase. His customers would love this game. The store had been open for only a few minutes when Milo's first set of customers walked in. It was a woman with her daughter. While Caroline spoke to the customer, Milo played with the teenager. Milo chased the ball a few times before it rolled under one of the glass shelves. Oh no! It happened again! The puppy immediately started to cry. The girl reached under the shelf and grabbed the ball. Milo stopped crying. He was a happy Chow again.

The customers finished with their purchases and left. By this point, Milo was ready for a snack, which he quickly ate and then went off to curl up in his new bed. He had earned a long nap, which he would enjoy in the quiet space by the front desk. Milo drifted to sleep dreaming of his life as a store mascot. A smile appeared on his face. The Chow's eyes were firmly closed. He continued to dream. Milo really enjoyed his job. He knew that he was doing important work and felt very good about himself.

He was a happy boy with an important job. Life was good for this Chow.

The Adventures
of Milo Chow...

Milo Chow, Superstar

abruptly. Milo looked up and immediately saw what his mum had seen. The letters M-I-L-O had been spray-painted onto their neighbours' fence. Milo couldn't believe it. He just couldn't believe it! His name wasn't just on collars and mugs, now it was on a fence! He looked at his mum. She must be so proud of him. Milo was also very proud of himself. He breathed in deeply and closed his eyes. A few seconds passed before he felt the familiar tug on his leash. It was time to continue on their walk. Milo walked very slowly, swaying from side to side. He knew that he was meant to focus on walking straight but the young Chow was too distracted. Caroline watched Milo for another minute before realising that at this speed she would be an old woman before they got home. She stopped and lifted the puppy into her arms. They continued towards home.

Once back at the house, Milo strolled into the kitchen. He wanted to have another look at all of the items that his mum had brought home. He sniffed each one again. He was still confused. Why did she have these things?

Caroline had been watching Milo with great amusement. His mum sat on the ground next to him believing that he understood every word that she uttered. In a very gentle voice Caroline told Milo that the collar, mug, placemat and bowl were all being used to raise money for the rescue that had saved him. He thought about that for a minute and came to one conclusion . . . MILO WAS A STAR!!!!

He was happy. Life was good for this Chow.

The Real Story of Milo

The Adventures of Milo Chow was written in honour of our real Chow Chow, Milo. He was born on November 3, 2019, in Manitoba, Canada, and sold by a breeder to a young couple who were either ill-equipped to deal with a special needs puppy or lacked the desire to make such a commitment. No diagnosis had been made when Milo left their home. His vet in Manitoba felt that he was aggressive and that the best thing to do was to euthanize the puppy. Milo was never aggressive towards us. The notion of this sweet pup being aggressive is simply laughable.

The buyers of this puppy agreed to surrender him to Mattie's Place, a rescue located in Toronto. Milo was given a second chance at health and happiness. The flight from Manitoba to Toronto took place on February 28, 2020. Milo was flown by Flights for Hope and collected by Denise Angus, owner of Mattie's Place, in the very early hours of February

29, 2020. She brought him back to her home to rest before bringing him into the rescue to meet his foster mum.

It took several attempts to reach his potential foster before it was clear that she was not interested in having Milo. I had been fortunate to be volunteering in Mattie's Place Retail for Rescue when Milo was brought in. After spending close to an hour with him in my arms and realising that this young boy had no place to go, I suggested that he come home with me. I remember being questioned by Denise about why I felt I was a suitable candidate to be Milo's foster mum. I guess I made my case.

Milo was almost four months old when he came into our care. He arrived underweight and with a terrible ear infection. We had hoped that antibiotics would treat the infection but also stabilise Milo so he no longer walked in circles. He did improve, but the circles never completely disappeared. He was diagnosed with hydrocephalus in July of 2020, following an MRI. The hope was that with treatment, Milo would still be able to have an excellent quality of life. It was agreed that if the initial treatment didn't work, a shunt would be used to remove the fluid around his brain. It was at this time that I was asked again about adopting the pup. I had two choices: keep him or let him be put up for adoption. I couldn't imagine our boy being with someone else.

The announcement of our decision to adopt Milo was posted on the Mattie's Place Facebook page on August 2, the anniversary of Sully's Gotcha Day. It was a very happy day.

On August 17, 2020, Milo woke up at 5:30 and was clearly very ill. I called Denise immediately and it was obvious that Milo needed to see his vet urgently. I walked out of the vet's office without my beloved Chow. There was nothing that could have been done. Milo was euthanized. Our hearts were broken.

Milo left a lasting impact on us. Our family, including the Mattie's Place family, continues to grieve his passing. We spent five-and-a-half incredible months with our boy and thankfully have a lifetime of memories to enjoy.

The Adventures of Milo Chow tells his story. This is him. We are forever indebted to Mattie's Place for saving the lives of countless pets, including Milo's brother, Sully, and sister,

Dominica. Although Milo's life was cut short, he lived those five months knowing that he was loved by us. I wouldn't have given that up for the world.

We cherished our time with this beautiful boy. This collection is for you, Milo. We love you today and forever.

Caroline Rayfield
(Milo Chow's mum)

Acknowledgements

The author would like to acknowledge the work done by Denise Angus and her rescue, Mattie's Place. Without the work done by Mattie's Place, Milo would never have had this story to tell.

Manufactured by Amazon.ca
Bolton, ON